emile and the field

words by
Kevin Young

art by
Chioma Ebinama

MAKE ME A WORLD
New York

There was a boy
named Emile

who fell
in love with a field.

It was wide
and blue—
and if you could have
seen it

so would've you.

He would whisper
to it for hours
and it would bring him
the yellowest flowers.

The bumblebees would sing
to him, never sting—
their words were honey,
which fed him

and led him
to wander.

His favorite maple
was tall as his mother—
taller than the other trees
who hid the field
and filled it with shade
and breeze.

One day
he began asking
if the field knew
what all it was missing—

it didn't know
the sea,

or skyscrapers—

it didn't know airplanes
(up close at least).

But the field did know fall—

knew how many stars
there were
and just how far—

it knew even the ones
bright but long gone.

Emile would ask his father,
What did the field know
of weather?

Where did it go
when covered over
by winter?

Emile hated how the snow
that fell there meant
Emile had to share
the field with sleds

and other, loud kids
who rode the face
of the field without
Emile's say-so.

Though they too
love it, and if we share,
Emile's father said,
who usually
had an answer,
and learn to take care,
it means the field
will be here
forever.

Emile thought
and thought—

he liked that idea
a lot. The field
would not, could not
be bought! or belong
to anyone.

Even Emile. Even him.

Besides, soon it would be spring
and the bees begin
again to sing.

To my great-grandfather Emile, who lent his name;
and to Mack, my son & inspiration
—K.Y.

To those I call family far and wide; past, future, and present
—C.E.

MAKE ME A WORLD is an imprint dedicated to exploring the vast possibilities of contemporary childhood. We strive to imagine a universe in which no young person is invisible, in which no kid's story is erased, in which no glass ceiling presses down on the dreams of a child. Then we publish books for that world, where kids ask hard questions and we struggle with them together, where dreams stretch from eons ago into the future and we do our best to provide road maps to where these young folks want to be. We make books where the children of today can see themselves and each other. When presented with fences, with borders, with limits, with all the kinds of chains that hobble imaginations and hearts, we proudly say—no.

Text copyright © 2022 by Kevin Young
Jacket art and interior illustrations copyright © 2022 by Chioma Ebinama

All rights reserved. Published in the United States by Make Me a World,
an imprint of Random House Children's Books, a division of Penguin Random House LLC, New York.

Make Me a World and the colophon are registered trademarks of Penguin Random House LLC.

Visit us on the Web! rhcbooks.com

Educators and librarians, for a variety of teaching tools, visit us at RHTeachersLibrarians.com

Library of Congress Cataloging-in-Publication Data is available upon request.
ISBN 978-1-9848-5042-3 (trade) | ISBN 978-1-9848-5043-0 (lib. bdg.) | ISBN 978-1-9848-5044-7 (ebook)

The text of this book is set in 18-point Filosofia.
The illustrations were created using watercolor and ink.
Book design by Nicole de las Heras

MANUFACTURED IN CHINA
March 2022
10 9 8 7 6 5 4 3 2 1
First Edition

MAKE ME A WORLD

Dear Reader,

As a city child, they would often take us to visit nature. Sometimes it was our school, sometimes another organization, but they would rent vans and pack us all in. They would drive us hours away from the concrete, glass, and pavement of our homes to various state parks and forests. Sometimes there would be a lake, or a trail, or an obstacle course with ropes and tires. Then, as sun was setting, they would pack us back into the van and take us home. I remember it felt random and strange. At the end, one of the adults would ask hopefully, "Did you guys have a good time in nature?"

It took me years to see what those nice people were awkwardly trying to show me. There is a gift to being in different spaces. There is a way the earth can talk to you. You can talk to the planet, to the green of it, to the sounds of water on the lake or of leaves. You can be part of the larger conversation that we as people have been having with the world since forever. You can talk with Basho, winding his way on Japan's seventeenth-century narrow roads, or sit with Thoreau by his New England pond, or wend your way through deserts with Mary Hunter Austin.

This book, here, is a conversation like that, with one of our great contemporary poets, essayists, and keepers of culture, Kevin Young. Kevin is the kind of guy who has been in many different spaces, from his work curating and caring for African American archives to his various fascinations with contemporary art and the uniquely American history of lies. A wide-ranging thinker like him needs a certain kind of ground, a certain centeredness. He shares a little part of that center in this story, *Emile and the Field*.

Kevin takes us on a field trip of sorts, alongside a young fine artist, Chioma Ebinama, whose work knows about margins and centers. The kind of trip that reminds me of all that is good in nature, the ease, the sweetness, the long conversation. The kind of trip I wish I could have given the city kid I was, being trundled onto buses to see . . . I didn't know what. With a book like this, I might have figured it out.

Christopher Myers